Jim Meets The Thing

Story by **Miriam Cohen**
Pictures by **Lillian Hoban**

A Young Yearling Book

Published by
Dell Publishing
a division of
Bantam Doubleday Dell Publishing Group, Inc.
666 Fifth Avenue
New York, New York 10103

The trademark Yearling® is registered in the U.S. Patent and Trademark Office.

The trademark Dell® is registered in the U.S. Patent and Trademark Office.

ISBN: 0-440-40149-6

Reprinted by arrangement with Greenwillow Books, a division of William Morrow & Company, Inc.

Printed in the United States of America

March 1989

10   9   8   7   6   5

W

FOR SUSAN

When Jim saw The Thing on television, he got scared. Maybe The Thing could come out of the TV!

He dreamed about it all night, and in
the morning he was still scared.

But when he came to school,
everybody was saying, "Did you see
The Thing?" "I did!" "I did!"

Danny said, "It was great. I loved it!"

"The Thing is so strong," Willy said, "if it just does like this with its eyes, the whole mountain falls down."
"But Captain Mighty can beat it," said Danny.

And Anna Maria said, "I liked it when
The Thing swallowed the car with four
people in it."
"Don't talk about it," Jim said.

"Uh-oh, Jim is scared!" Danny shouted.

"No, I'm not," Jim tried to tell everybody.
But nobody listened.

At lunch, Jim didn't feel like eating his little bag of Chee-Tees. He couldn't stop thinking about The Thing.

Why was he the only one in first grade who got scared?

Paul said, "Come on, Jim, let's play."

"Let's play Super Heroes on TV," said Anna Maria. "I'll be Gravity Girl. Paul can be my husband, Web Man." Paul didn't want to, but George said he would.

Danny said, "I'll be Captain Mighty."
"Who are you going to be, Jim?"
Margaret asked.

Jim shook his head.
He didn't feel like a Super Hero.

Anna Maria jumped from the sixth bar of the jungle gym. She jumped in front of Louie and Margaret.

"Don't try to get away! I'll just turn on my gravity belt and you'll be stuck!" she shouted. Jim walked away. He could only jump from the fourth bar.

George was pretending to throw webs
all over the playground. He worked
very hard. Danny jumped on the lunch
table bench. "Captain Mighty!" he
shouted.

"Stop that, Danny!" Margaret was mad.
"I was eating my tuna fish sandwich with
teeny tiny bites and you made me make
a mistake!"

"I can't stop. I'm too strong!" Danny grabbed
one hand in his other hand and pulled till his
face turned red.

"There is something walking on you, Danny,"
said Sara.

"There is not," said Danny. Then he said,

"What is it?"

"I think it is a praying mantis," said Sara.

"HELP! HELP! Get it off!" Danny yelled.

"I'm not going to touch it," said Anna Maria.
Paul said, "Its arms are like green sticks
with pincers."

"Its eyes are like the lights in front of a car," said Danny.
And Willy said, "That bug is mean!"
"You'd better run, man!"
shouted Sammy.

But Jim said, "Stay still, Danny."
He took a piece of paper and put it
under the praying mantis. Then he
carefully lifted the praying mantis
off Danny.

Everybody moved back. "Yuck!"
"Squash it!" "Kill it!" the kids screamed.
"No," said Jim. And George said, "How
would you like it if somebody squashed
you?"

Jim took the praying mantis to the corner of the playground and put a leaf on top of it.

The lunch bell rang and they went in for
gymnastics. "Boy, you weren't even
scared. You must be Mantis Man!"
Willy told Jim.

Sammy stood on his head. "I wasn't
scared either. But you know what I *am*
scared of? Sometimes I think robbers
could come out of the toilet."
"I don't think they could," said Sara.

George was doing the bicycle. "I used to be scared of Dracula all the time, but now I'm not," he said.

And Paul told them, "When I was a little kid, I was scared. I thought Web Man was bad. But now I know he's good."

Suddenly Jim did a double flipper somersault. He jumped up. Everyone in first grade got scared sometimes. But he wasn't scared now. Mantis Man could beat The Thing!